for
Alexander
Blake
Masser
McKimmie
and
my
brothers
and
sisters

Brian Banana Duck Sunshine Yellow

Chris McKimmie

ALLEN&UNWIN

I have three first names. Brian Banana and Duck. My last name is Yellow. This is my room at Na-na and Grumpy Yellow's place.

Na-na and Grumpy Yellow live in the other room.

Na-na calls me Banana and Grumpy calls me Duck.

I stay with them Friday nights, all day Saturday and most of Sunday.

I like it when we go to the lake and I swim with the other ducks.

'Don't go too far out, Banana,'
Na-na calls.

One Saturday morning
Na-na put on
her face.
We got in
the
lift
t● go
d
o
w
n
t● the
shops.
'Duck,'
said Grumpy,
'don't f●rget
the fish
and chips.'

Na-na panicked when I hid in the bananas.

Where is my Banana?
Where is my darling Banana?'
she thought I was lost.

People
thought
she was nuts.

Then I did get lost.
My name was
    called over the
    supermarket loudspeaker.

'Check, 1, 2, 3...is this thing on?'
NA-NA HAS LOST HER BANANA.

A big prawn found me
    near the seafood
    and
    took me to
    the lost and
        found.

'Never again,
    Brian,'
Na-na said.
'That's it.'

She
made
me
carry a
yellow
balloon
so
I
would
never
get
lost
again.

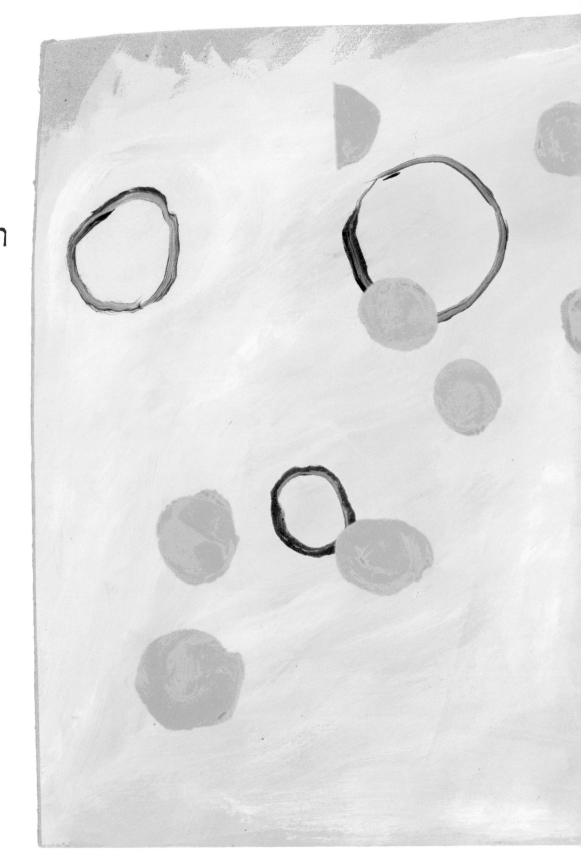

Real
ducks
don't
carry
balloons.
(Not even yellow ones.)

At home Grumpy was watching footy on Tv.

'Go the Saints!' he yelled.

'Go Ducks!' I yelled.

'Duck,' said Grumpy, 'there is no footy team called the Ducks.'

'GOOOOO DUCKS!' I yelled.

'GOOOOO!'

'Grumpy,' hissed Na-na. 'Take Brian **OUT** for the afternoon.

We
went
to
see
the
big
cow

again.

'Duck,' said Grumpy, 'the **big** cow is five times **bigger** than a real cow.'

'What about the **big** duck?' I said.

'Brian,'
said Grumpy,
'there is
no
big
duck.'

A strong wind lifted me up.

'Come back, come back, Duck!' Grumpy called.

I coul

...ee forever.

I saw
the **big duck.**

'It's
just
beautiful,
Wayne!'

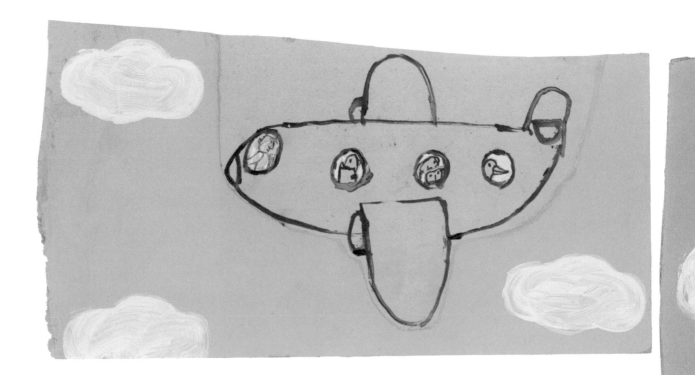

I took it home.

'Hey,
you!
Bring
it
back!'

Na-na
and
Grumpy
said,

'Of
course
you
can
keep
it,
Sunshine.'

I
like
being

a
Yellow.

Allen & Unwin
83 Alexander St
Crows Nest NSW 2065
Australia
Phone: (61 2) 84 25 0100
fax: (61 2) 9906 2218
Email: info@allenandunwin.com
Web: www.allenandunwin.com

National Library of Australia
Cataloguing-in-Publication entry:
McKimmie, Chris.
Brian Banana Duck Sunshine Yellow.
For children.
ISBN 1 741 14 741 7.
1.Title
A823.3

Book design, font design and
Lettering
Chris McKimmie

The text of this book
is set in
dylanandblake.

Printed in Singapore
by Tien Wah Press.
10 9 8 7 6 5 4 3 2 1

The pictures are
done with acrylic
paint on mdf board
and paper. Some are
drawn on paper
with ink.

www.chrismckimmie.com